This book
belongs to

Alexandra

Other books by Mick Inkpen:

KIPPER

KIPPER'S TOYBOX

KIPPER'S BIRTHDAY

ONE BEAR AT BEDTIME

THE BLUE BALLOON

THREADBEAR

BILLY'S BEETLE

PENGUIN SMALL

WHERE, OH WHERE, IS KIPPER'S BEAR?

British Library Cataloguing in Publication data

A catalogue record for this book is available from
the British Library

ISBN 0 340 62686 0

Text and illustrations copyright © Mick Inkpen 1993

The right of Mick Inkpen to be identified as the author of this work
has been asserted by him in accordance with
the Copyright, Designs and Patents Act 1988.

First published 1993

This edition published 1995

9 8 7 6 5 4 3 2 1

Published by Hodder Children's Books,
a division of Hodder Headline Plc
338 Euston Road
London NW1 3BH

Printed in Italy by L.E.G.O., Vicenza

Lullabyhullaballoo!

Mick Inkpen

*Hodder
Children's
Books*

a division of Hodder Headline plc

The sun is down.
The moon is up.
It is bedtime for the
Little Princess.
But outside the castle...

A dragon is roaring.
What shall we do?
He's hissing and snorting!
What shall we do?
We'll tell him to SSSH!
That's what we'll do.

SSSH!

YES YOU!

But,

The brave knights are clanking.

What shall we do?

They're rattling and clunking!

What shall we do?

We'll tell them to SSSH!

That's what we'll do.

SSSH!

YES YOU!

But,

The ghosts are oooooing.
What shall we do?
They're ooo ooo oooooing!
What shall we do?
We'll tell them to SSSH!
That's what we'll do.

SSSH!

But,

The giant is stamping.

What shall we do?

He's galumphing and stomping!

What shall we do?

We'll tell him to SSSH!

That's what we'll do.

SSSH!

YES YOOOOOOOO!

YES DO!

But,

Out in the forest

Wolves are howling

Owls are hooting

Frogs are croaking

Mice are squeaking

Bats are flapping

Bears are growling

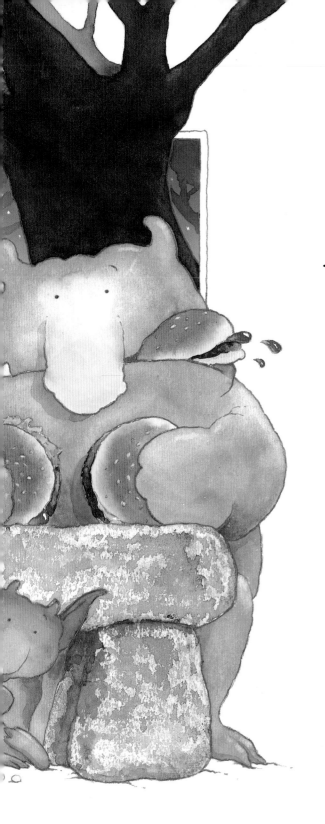

And the trolls
and the goblins
are guzzling
and gobbling
and slurping
and burping!

What shall we do?

We'll tell them to ...

...STOP!

But now,
The Princess is crying!
What shall we do?
She won't stop howling!
What shall we do?
We'll sing her a lullaby.
That's what we'll do.
We'll ALL sing a lullaby.

Now the Princess is smiling.

Her eyelids are drooping.

The Princess is sleeping.

So what shall we do?
We'll tiptoe to bed
And we shall sleep too.
We shall sleep too.

But,

snore!

snore!

nore!

snore!

snore!

snore!

snore!

…the Princess is snoring!
What *shall* we do?

snor

snore!